PUFFIN BOOKS

The Surprise Party

Willow exchanged excited looks with
Troy and Storm. A surprise
birthday party! She couldn't wait until
the three of them were on their
own and they could start to plan it.
This was going to be fun!

Linda Chapman lives in Leicestershire with her family and two Bernese mountain dogs. She used to be a stage manager in the theatre. When she is not writing she spends her time looking after her two young daughters, horse riding and teaching drama. You can find out more about Linda on her website lindachapman.co.uk or visit mysecretunicorn.co.uk

Unicorn School

The Surprise Party

Linda Chapman

Illustrated by Ann Kronheimer

PUFFIN

PUFFIN BOOKS

Published by the Penguin Group
Penguin Books Ltd, 80 Strand, London WC2R ORL, England
Penguin Group (USA) Inc., 375 Hudson Street, New York, New York 10014, USA
Penguin Group (Canada), 90 Eglinton Avenue East, Suite 700, Toronto, Ontario, Canada M4P 2Y3
(a division of Pearson Penguin Canada Inc.)
Penguin Ireland, 25 St Stephen's Green, Dublin 2, Ireland (a division of Penguin Books Ltd)
Penguin Group (Australia), 250 Camberwell Road, Camberwell, Victoria 3124, Australia
(a division of Pearson Australia Group Pty Ltd)
Penguin Books India Pvt Ltd, 11 Community Centre, Panchsheel Park,
New Delhi – 110 017, India
Penguin Group (NZ), 67 Apollo Drive, Rosedale, North Shore 0632, New Zealand
(a division of Pearson New Zealand Ltd)
Penguin Books (South Africa) (Pty) Ltd, 24 Sturdee Avenue, Rosebank,
Johannesburg 2196, South Africa

Penguin Books Ltd, Registered Offices: 80 Strand, London WC2R ORL, England

puffinbooks.com

First published 2007
2

Text copyright © Working Partners Ltd, 2007
Illustrations copyright © Ann Kronheimer, 2007
All rights reserved

The moral right of the author and illustrator has been asserted

Set in Bembo
Typeset by Palimpsest Book Production Limited, Grangemouth, Stirlingshire
Made and printed in England by Clays Ltd, St Ives plc

British Library Cataloguing in Publication Data
A CIP catalogue record for this book is available from the British Library

ISBN: 978-0-141-32248-3

To Jemima Young

ARCADIA

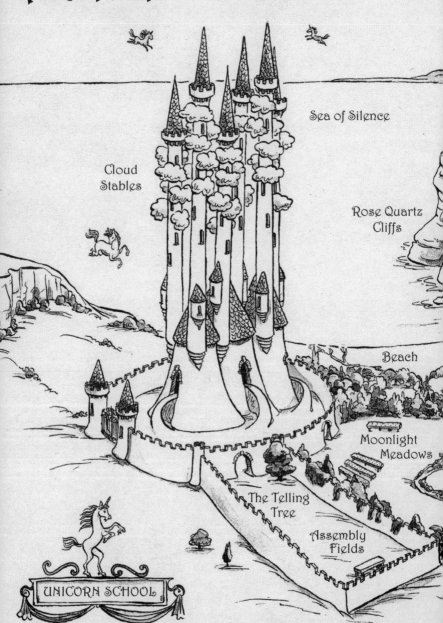

Sea of Silence

Cloud
Stables

Rose Quartz
Cliffs

Beach

Moonlight
Meadows

The Telling
Tree

Assembly
Fields

UNICORN SCHOOL

Contents

Chapter One

Willow's Great Idea

Willow trotted across the grass towards the Charm Fields. She didn't want to be late for her lesson. The sky was blue and the sunshine glittered on her golden horn. A little way ahead of her she spotted one of her best friends, Sapphire.

'Sapphire! Wait!' Willow called.

Sapphire turned. She was a very pretty unicorn with a mane and tail that swept almost to the ground, a slender silver horn and big eyes fringed by long dark eyelashes.

Willow cantered up to her. 'Hi!'

'Hello,' Sapphire muttered.

Willow frowned. Her friend looked sad. 'Are you OK?'

'Yes.' But there was a definite sigh

in Sapphire's voice and her ears weren't pricked forward as they usually were. 'I'm just feeling a bit homesick, that's all,' she admitted.

Willow touched noses with her. Unicorns who lived in the magic land of Arcadia went to boarding school when they were nine years old to learn how to use their magic. Willow and Sapphire had both started school a month ago. Willow missed her mum and dad and two older brothers too, but she loved being at Unicorn School so much that she never felt homesick for long. However, Willow knew Sapphire was different and that there were days when she really missed being at home with her six brothers and sisters.

'It's probably because I've been thinking about my birthday next Sunday,' Sapphire went on. 'It's going to be really strange not being at home for it. Whenever one of us has a birthday all the others put on a show for them. Everyone does magic tricks and then we have a big birthday cake. It's really good fun.' She shook her head. 'Oh, I'm just being silly, Willow. My birthday will be fine. Come on! If we don't get going, we'll be late for our charms lesson.' She broke into a canter as if she didn't want to talk about it any more.

Willow plunged forward beside her, but she couldn't stop thinking about what Sapphire had just said. She felt awful that Sapphire might be sad on her birthday. *I wish I could do something*, she thought. *But what?*

Storm and Troy, Willow and Sapphire's other best friends, were already in the Charm Fields, standing with the rest of the Year Ones. All the unicorns at Unicorn School belonged to one of four houses – they were in Rainbow House, Star House, Moon House or Sun House. Storm, Troy, Willow and Sapphire were in Rainbow House. It meant that they ate their meals together at the same table and slept in the same stable, but they did their lessons with all the other Year Ones from the different houses.

'Hi!' Storm neighed as Willow and Sapphire cantered over. He was a tall unicorn with a silvery-white horn, straight nose and a thick dark mane and tail. Willow, who was very small for nine, looked tiny beside him.

'Have you heard we're going to make a new type of charm today?' said Troy, a handsome, athletic unicorn with an arched neck. 'It makes the person who has the charm feel very brave.'

'That sounds fun,' Willow said. She

looked at Sapphire, but Sapphire was lost in her own thoughts. Willow wondered if she was still thinking about her birthday.

I wonder if Troy and Storm can help me think of something we can do to make Sapphire's birthday special, she thought.

Just then Damaris, the charms teacher, came trotting into the field. 'Hello, class,' she said, smiling around at them all. 'Today I'm going to

teach you how to make a courage charm.' A buzz of excitement ran round the Year Ones. 'Can you get into pairs, please?'

Willow paired up with Sapphire, and Troy paired up with Storm. Sometimes Willow and Storm were partners, but she and Troy had learnt that they didn't get on well as a pair because they both liked being in charge and tended to argue a lot!

Damaris handed out two silver hearts to each pair and then gave them instructions for making the heart into a courage charm.

'You must wind a hair from your mane around your charm. Touch the charm three times with your horn, each time thinking about someone doing something brave, and then say: *Be brave. Stand strong. Take courage with you.* You will know the spell has worked when your charm glows with a red light.'

Willow was good at charms and her metal heart was soon glowing a faint red colour. But it was nowhere near as impressive as Troy's. His shone like a bright red light.

'Well done,' said Damaris approvingly. 'You must have been thinking some very brave thoughts, Troy.' She moved on through the rest of the class.

'What were you thinking about, Troy?' Sapphire asked.

'I was thinking about some of the things my dad did when he was younger. He did all sorts of brave things before he became the . . .' Troy broke off suddenly.

'Became the what?' said Willow curiously. Troy didn't have any brothers or sisters and he had never really talked much about his parents.

'Nothing,' Troy muttered, looking unusually flustered. 'Um, Storm, your charm has started to glow!' He went over to Storm's charm.

'Hey, it has!' Storm said, looking pleased.

'Well done, Storm,' Sapphire said, nuzzling him. She sighed. 'I think I'd better go and ask Damaris about my charm. It's not glowing even a little bit.' She hurried after the teacher.

Storm snorted. 'Did you two know it's Sapphire's birthday next Sunday?'

Willow and Troy nodded.

'She's sad that she's not going to be at home for her birthday,' Willow said. 'Her brothers and sisters usually put on a show for her where they all do magic tricks and then they have a big birthday cake.'

'Poor Sapphire,' said Troy in concern.

'It's a pity her brothers and sisters can't come here to do a show for her,' said Storm.

Willow stared. Storm's words had

just given her a brilliant idea! '*They* can't come here, but *we'll* be here! Why don't *we* do a show for her?'

'Oh, yes!' Storm exclaimed.

'It would be cool!' said Troy.

'We could make it into a surprise birthday party,' Willow went on, her mind buzzing. 'We can practise when Sapphire goes to the quartz-gazing club.'

'OK,' the other two agreed. Sapphire had recently joined the quartz-gazing club where they practised their unicorn magic to use rocks of rose quartz to see other people and places.

Just then Sapphire came trotting back. 'I forgot to think of *three* brave things,' she told them. 'I only thought of two.' She went back over to her charm to try again.

Willow exchanged excited looks with Troy and Storm. A surprise birthday party! She couldn't wait until the three of them were on their own and they could start to plan it. This was going to be fun!

Exciting News

When the charms lesson
had finished Willow and
the other Year One unicorns
went to the Flying Heath. Atlas,
their flying teacher, had some
news for them. 'Next Sunday
it will be the monthly flying
race.'

'That's on my birthday,' Sapphire whispered to Willow.

'I've heard about that,' Troy put in eagerly. 'There's a race once a month and the winners get medals, don't they?'

Atlas nodded.

'Can anyone go in the race?' asked Moondust, a unicorn from Star House.

'No, there are qualifying heats,' Atlas explained. 'The unicorns who come first, second or third in each heat qualify to take part in the race. Usually it's just the older unicorns who are allowed to take part in the heats, but if I think that a younger unicorn is good enough at flying then they are allowed to go in the heats too, if they want to.' He looked round at them all. 'This month I think one of you *is* good enough.'

'Who?' asked several of them.

'Troy,' announced Atlas.

Troy gave a whinny of joy. 'Me?'

Willow, Sapphire and Storm exchanged delighted looks. Troy was brilliant at flying. Most unicorns

didn't learn to fly properly until they came to Unicorn School, but Troy had already learnt at home.

'You are a very fast, very strong flyer,' Atlas told him. 'If you would like to take part in the heats tomorrow, you may.'

'Yes, please!' Troy exclaimed. 'My dad's told me all about the races he went in when he was at school here. He used to win all the time!'

Atlas smiled at him. 'Then come to the Flying Heath at ten o'clock tomorrow morning.' He looked around at the others. 'The rest of you are all very welcome to come and watch and support. Now let's get started on today's lesson. We are going to be practising swooping and diving. Can you all line up, please?'

As everyone lined up, Willow turned to Troy. 'That's great news!'

'Thanks!' Troy said.

'You'll be the only Year One in the heats,' Storm said, looking awestruck. 'That's amazing, Troy.'

'Thanks,' Troy said smugly. 'I am quite good at flying, aren't I?'

'And modest too!' Willow said, prodding him sharply with her horn.

'Ow!' Troy snorted. He looked a bit shamefaced. 'OK, OK. I'm sorry. I guess that did sound a bit big-headed.'

Willow grinned at him. Troy sometimes did boast a bit about

how good he was at sports and flying, but he usually realized it and said sorry. 'I bet you get into the main flying race and do really well,' she told him.

He looked at her gratefully. 'Thanks, Willow.'

'Quiet, everyone!' Atlas called. 'Let's get started!'

Atlas made them fly really high and then practise swooping as fast as they could towards the ground. It was the last lesson of the day and afterwards Sapphire went off to her quartz-gazing club.

'Let's get together and work out a plan for the party!' Willow told

Storm and Troy. They found a quiet corner of Moonlight Meadows and, in between taking mouthfuls of the sweet green grass, they talked about Sapphire's birthday.

'My mum will send a cake if I ask her,' Troy said, swishing his tail. 'I'll get her to send a really big one, three layers, covered in pink and white icing with ten candles and a sugar unicorn that looks like Sapphire on the top.'

'That sounds like it might be very hard to make,' Storm said.

'Oh, don't worry about that,' said Troy airily. 'Mum will just get one of the elves to make it for her.'

'One of the *elves*?' Willow echoed.

Only a very few, very important unicorns, like the Unicorn Elders who ruled Arcadia, had elves working for them.

'Your parents have got elves?' Storm said.

Looking a bit flustered, Troy nodded. 'Yeah.'

Willow and Storm stared at him.

'It's not a big deal,' mumbled Troy, looking as if he wished he hadn't said anything.

'So are your mum and dad Unicorn Elders?' Willow asked curiously.

'No,' said Troy quickly. 'Look, I thought we were supposed to be talking about Sapphire's birthday. What about the show?

What are we going to do for it?'

It was obvious he was trying to change the subject. Willow hesitated for a moment, but then decided not to press him further. 'Well, I thought we could do magic tricks like Sapphire's brothers and sisters usually do,' she replied. 'I'm going to practise magicking rainbow-coloured stars with my horn.'

Willow was good at making stars appear. 'Maybe I can make them come out in letters that spell out *Happy birthday, Sapphire!*'

'That sounds fantastic! And I could do a flying display,' said Troy. Willow prodded him with her horn before he could say anything boastful. 'Ow!' he said, looking hurt. 'I didn't mean I could just show off. I could spell out *Happy birthday, Sapphire* in the sky, doing some somersaults and dives.'

Willow felt a bit bad for prodding him. 'That's a really good idea!' she said enthusiastically. 'I bet Sapphire would love it!'

'What can I do?' asked Storm.

Willow thought for a moment. Storm was extremely strong, but that wasn't something that could really be used in a party trick. What else was he good at? Suddenly she remembered how good he was at doing magic with water. At school all the unicorns learnt how to purify water, but Storm could also make it change colour.

'I know!' she said. 'Why don't you do some of your water magic?'

'OK!' said Storm eagerly. 'We could have the party on the beach and I could make one of the rock pools change colour.'

'Let's get practising!' Troy exclaimed.

They began. Troy was soon somersaulting in the sky and doing some of the steepest dives Willow had ever seen as he tried to work out how to do the letters to spell out:

Happy birthday,
Sapphire

Willow managed to get stars in all the colours of the rainbow one after the other. It was hard to get them to go into the shape of the letters in *Happy birthday, Sapphire*, but she kept trying. Storm changed the water in a nearby silver water trough into all the colours of the rainbow too, one after another.

'We could all do our magic together,' said Willow as she made violet stars appear at the same time as Storm made the water turn violet. 'We'd have to practise loads, but I bet Sapphire would love it! We can practise whenever she's at her club.'

The other two unicorns nodded. Just then the chief elf came into the meadows and blew a clear note on a large white shell. Elves came bustling through the golden gates to the meadows with four tables. Each table had a series of circular holes down its sides and other elves came out carrying buckets of bran, apples, oats and carrots that they placed in the holes for the unicorn pupils to eat from.

'It's teatime!' Willow said to Storm and Troy. 'Come on!'

They headed over to the Rainbow House table. They had just reached it when Sapphire and the other unicorns in the quartz-gazing club came cantering into the meadows.

'Hi!' Sapphire said, slipping into the place beside Willow.

'How was quartz-gazing?' Willow asked her.

'Great!' Sapphire enthused. 'I managed to look into a rose-quartz rock and use my magic to see my house and my parents! What have you been up to?'

'Oh, nothing,' Willow said quickly. She grinned to herself. If only Sapphire knew they'd been practising a birthday surprise for her!

The food was delicious. Troy asked for second then third helpings.

'You'll be too heavy to fly in the heat tomorrow if you have any more,' Willow teased him.

Troy didn't bother to reply, but just gobbled up the last apple out of her bowl and looked at her smugly as she snorted in annoyance.

'Right, for that I'm not coming to support you tomorrow!' she declared, pretending to be cross.

Troy grinned at her, but when she kept the cross look on her face he began to look alarmed. 'You don't mean it, do you? You're not really cross with me, Willow? You will come, won't you?'

'Of course I will, silly!' she said, butting him with her head.

'We'll all be there,' Sapphire told him.

'We wouldn't miss it for anything,' said Storm.

'I'm really nervous,' Troy admitted. 'I *so* want to do well. My dad told me he used to win the monthly flying race all the time when he was here. He was the fastest unicorn at school. I hope I do OK in the heats.'

Willow nuzzled him. 'You will. I know you will!'

The Bronze
Scroll

The following morning nearly all the unicorns in the school gathered for the heats on the Flying Heath. It was a flat area of short grass with a few trees and bramble bushes. Willow stood at the edge of it with Storm and Sapphire. 'Oh, I hope Troy does OK,' she said. She and Troy might tease each other a lot, but she really wanted him to do well in the heats. She felt almost as nervous as if she was going in them herself!

Sapphire snorted anxiously. 'He'll be really upset if he doesn't qualify for the main race. You heard what he said about his dad winning races when he was at school.'

'He *will* qualify,' said Storm stoutly. 'I know he will.'

Atlas led all the unicorns who were going to be racing on to the heath. Troy was the smallest unicorn in the group, but he held his head proudly and lifted his knees high as he walked out beside the older unicorns.

'What's he got round his neck?'
Willow said. Troy was wearing a
kind of sash made out of three
bright ribbons – one blue, one gold
and one red – plaited together.

'That's his lucky sash,' Storm told
her. 'He was telling me about it
yesterday. His mum gave it to him
and he always wears it when
something important is happening.

It's not magic, but he says wearing it always makes him feel lucky.'

Willow noticed that some of the other unicorns had ribbons round their necks or tied in their manes or round their tails too. 'I hope it *does* bring him luck,' she said.

Atlas led the racing unicorns over to the starting point where there was a golden chain hung between two trees. The chief elf was standing by one of the trees with a conch shell. The unicorns in each heat had to stand behind the chain. When the elf blew the shell they had to fly over the chain, race round two trees and then get to the finish line at the other end of the heath.

There were going to be four heats in all. Troy was in the second heat. He and the other racing unicorns waited nervously while the first heat took place. Willow, Sapphire and Storm cheered for the unicorns they knew best. To their delight Juniper, who was a Year Six in Rainbow House, won easily and Oriel, a Year Three, came third.

Then it was Troy's turn to line up. He was between two Year Five unicorns from Moon House, Rowan and Emerald. Willow also recognized a Year Three called Sorrel and two Year Sixes from Star House: Cloud and Silver.

Oh, please let Troy do well, thought

Willow, swishing her tail anxiously. *Please, please, please!*

Troy looked over in their direction. 'Good luck!' they all whinnied as loudly as they could.

'Are you ready, everyone?' Atlas said. He waited until all the unicorns behind the chain were still and then nodded at the elf. The elf lifted the shell to his lips, blew a note and the unicorns in Troy's heat were off!

'Go on, Troy!' Storm neighed as the unicorns soared into the blue sky.

Silver took the lead. She was closely followed by Cloud, but Troy was only just behind them. Rowan and Sorrel tried to overtake him,

but Troy stuck his neck out and galloped even faster as he whizzed round the trees. He drew up alongside Cloud, passed him and began to gain on Silver as they approached the finish line.

Willow cantered up and down on the spot with excitement. 'He's going to win!' she neighed as Troy reached Silver's side. The finish line was approaching fast. But neither

Silver nor Cloud wanted to be beaten. They both flew even faster. For a minute all three unicorns were racing along, neck and neck, but then Silver and Cloud just began to edge ahead. Silver thrust her muzzle forward and dived across the finish line ahead of Cloud with Troy in third place.

'He's in the final!' Sapphire squealed.

'Let's go and congratulate him!' said Willow.

The three of them raced over to where the unicorns were flying to the ground. Their sides were heaving with the effort and their necks were damp with sweat.

'That was brilliant!' Willow whinnied to Troy.

'You're in the final!' Storm exclaimed.

Troy lifted his head. To Willow's surprise, he looked very disappointed. 'I was only third,' he panted.

'But you still qualified,' said Willow.

Sapphire nodded. 'And all the other unicorns were loads older than you.'

'You did *really* well,' Storm told him.

'No, I didn't,' Troy said. 'I didn't win.'

'Well done, everyone,' Atlas called.

'Now if you could all go over to one side, please, so we can have the next heat.'

They watched the last two heats together, but even when Troy got his breath back he didn't cheer up. Willow couldn't understand why he didn't seem to be happier that he had come third.

After the final heat the elf blew his horn for quiet and Atlas spoke to all the unicorns. 'Well done to everyone who took part. The Tricorn will now present scrolls to those who have qualified for the final a week on Sunday.'

'The Tricorn!' Willow whispered in awe. The Tricorn was the school's

Headmaster. He was a very old and wise unicorn with a horn striped in three colours – gold, silver and bronze.

The chief elf blew a fanfare on the shell and the Tricorn walked out on to the Flying Heath. Behind him was another elf carrying a mother-of-pearl tray with twelve rolled-up paper scrolls on it, four tied with gold ribbons, four tied with silver ribbons and four tied with bronze ribbons.

The Tricorn stopped next to Atlas and looked around at the watching unicorns with his wise dark eyes. 'Congratulations, everyone. Would the winners now come and collect their scrolls, please? From the first heat: in first place, Juniper; in second place, Azure; in third place, Oriel.'

The three unicorns whose names he had called walked out proudly. Juniper was given a scroll with a gold ribbon, Azure a scroll with a silver ribbon and Oriel a scroll with a bronze ribbon. They all looked very pleased.

When the second heat was announced and it was Troy's turn to go and get his scroll with a bronze ribbon, he hung his head and walked slowly up to the Tricorn. He only muttered a brief *thank you*. Willow saw the Tricorn look at him in surprise.

Troy came back looking dejected.

'Well done!' Sapphire whispered as the unicorns in the final two heats went up to get their scrolls.

'It's only a bronze scroll. What good is coming third?' Troy said unhappily.

'It *is* good,' Storm told him.

Troy shoved the scroll towards Storm. 'Here, you have it then if you think it's so good.'

'Troy!' Storm said in surprise. 'It's yours.'

'Well, I don't want it!' Troy threw the scroll on the ground and stamped on it angrily with his front hoof. 'Stupid third place! My dad would have won!'

'Troy!' Willow exclaimed. She glanced round and to her horror realized the Tricorn had seen what Troy had just done. He was heading towards them with a frown on his face. 'Oh, no!' she said in dismay. 'You're going to be in trouble now!'

'Troy!'

Troy jumped and looked round.

'Why did you just do that to your scroll?' the Tricorn asked.

Troy looked embarrassed. 'I . . . er . . .'

'Well?' the Tricorn insisted.

'I threw it on the floor because it was only a bronze scroll,' Troy admitted in a small voice. 'I wanted to win a gold one.'

The Tricorn shook his head. 'Oh, Troy. I am *very* disappointed in you. It is not winning that matters, but taking part and doing your best. You should be proud of what you achieved rather than sulking because you did not come first. I would expect any of the unicorns at school here to behave properly, but someone from your background should *certainly* act with more dignity and less foolishness. Your father would be very unhappy with you. Now pick up your scroll and do not let me see behaviour like this from you again.'

The Tricorn turned and walked away, his noble head held high. Slowly Troy picked the scroll off the ground.

Sapphire looked anxiously at him. 'Are you all right?'

'Yes,' he muttered, but he looked really upset.

'What did the Tricorn mean about someone from your background?' Storm asked curiously.

'I don't know,' said Troy quickly.

'He made it sound like you were special or something,' said Willow.

'Special! Me? No,' Troy stammered. 'I'm just normal. I'm . . . I'm just like all of you.'

Willow frowned. He was acting very strangely. 'What's going on, Troy? Is there something you're not telling us?'

'No! Just stop asking questions and leave me alone!' Troy stamped his front hooves crossly. And to their astonishment he turned and cantered away!

Troy's Secret

'Wait, Troy!' Willow called. She and the others hurried after him. There were so many unicorns about that he couldn't go far and they soon caught up with him.

'Why did you go off like that?' Sapphire asked him.

'What's wrong?' said Willow. 'I
didn't mean to upset you.'

For a moment Troy looked as if
he was about to tell them
something, but then he just sighed.
'I'm sorry about cantering away. I
guess I was just upset at being told
off. Let's go to the Moonlight
Meadows – it's almost lunchtime.'

Storm and Sapphire nodded, but
Willow was still concerned.

'Is everything really OK?' she asked.

'Yes,' he insisted. His eyes looked at her pleadingly. 'Can we just forget it, Willow? Please?'

He looked so unhappy that Willow nodded. 'OK, let's go to the meadows then.'

It can't be anything really important, she thought to herself as they headed down the cliff path, *or he'd tell us. We are his best friends.*

'What shall we do after lunch?' Storm asked.

'Well, at three o'clock I'm supposed to be meeting up with Topaz,' Sapphire replied. 'We're going to the Rose Quartz Cliffs.

I can see Topaz over there – I'll just go and check that she still wants to go.' She trotted on ahead.

Willow turned to the others. 'Should we practise for the birthday surprise while Sapphire's with Topaz this afternoon?'

'OK!' the other two replied eagerly.

After lunch Storm went up to the stables with Troy while Willow and Sapphire went to the beach together.

'Do you think Troy is really OK?' Willow asked Sapphire as they paddled in the crystal-clear Sea of Silence. The water sparkled as their hooves splashed through it. 'It *was* strange the way he cantered off like that this morning.'

'He was probably just feeling embarrassed about being told off,' Sapphire replied.

'Maybe.' Willow flicked her ears. 'You don't think that there's something he's not telling us, do you?'

'What sort of thing? We're his friends. He wouldn't keep anything secret from us,' said Sapphire.

Willow had to admit it didn't make sense. 'You're probably right,' she said. She looked at the calm sea stretching out ahead of them. 'Come on! Let's go for a gallop through the water!'

At three o'clock Topaz came to the beach to meet Sapphire, and Willow headed back to the Moonlight Meadows. Storm was waiting for her near a group of Year Three unicorns, but there was no sign of Troy.

'Where is he?' Willow puzzled after they had waited a few minutes. 'You don't think he's gone flying and has forgotten about our practice, do you?'

'I don't know,' said Storm. 'I know he was going to practise his racing starts earlier, but just as he was on his way out of the stables, one of the elves came and gave him a message. I asked Troy what it was about, but he said it wasn't important.'

'I guess we'll have to get started without him then,' said Willow.

'I'm sure he'll be here soon,' said Storm.

But Troy didn't turn up. Willow got crosser and crosser that he could have forgotten. She was so annoyed, her magic wouldn't work properly. The stars didn't flow into the right shapes and they were all

plain blue instead of being
rainbow-coloured.

'Oh, this is useless!' She stamped
her hoof after half an hour of
practising. 'Where is Troy?'

As the words left her mouth, Troy
came galloping across the meadows
towards them. 'Sorry I'm late,' he
panted as he came to a stop.

'Where have you been?' Willow
said. 'Were you out flying?'

'Of course not,' Troy said
indignantly. 'I wouldn't go flying if I
was supposed to be meeting you.'

'So what *have* you been doing?'
Storm asked.

Troy opened his mouth and then
shut it again. 'I . . . I can't say.'

'You can't say!' Willow stamped her hoof. 'What do you mean, you can't say?'

'I . . . I just can't,' Troy replied. Willow turned her back on him. The least he could do was tell them what had made him so late.

'Don't be cross, Willow,' Troy pleaded, pawing the ground anxiously. Willow didn't say anything.

Troy sighed. 'OK, look, I'll tell you why I was late, but you mustn't tell anyone else – well, apart from Sapphire.'

Willow's curiosity conquered her anger. She turned back round. 'So why were you late?'

'It's to do with my family.' Troy took a deep breath. 'There's something I haven't been telling you. You see my dad's the . . .' He hesitated. 'He's the King of Arcadia.' Willow and Storm stared at him.

'Your dad's the king?' said Storm slowly. 'So you're a . . .'

'*Prince!*' gasped Willow. 'You're the Prince of Arcadia! So, that's what the Tricorn meant about "someone from your background".'

Troy nodded. 'And it's why I couldn't come to practise with you just now. One of the elves brought me a message saying I had to go and see the Tricorn. The Tricorn's actually my great-uncle. He said my dad is coming on a visit soon and he wanted to know if I had decided to tell people I was the Prince of Arcadia or not. When I started school I said I wanted it to be a secret. I didn't want people to know and treat me differently.'

'I can't believe you didn't tell us,' said Willow.

'Yes, we're your best friends,' said Storm.

'I know, I know. I should have told you. But it was hard,' Troy replied, his voice rising. 'I just didn't know how to suddenly tell you that my dad is the King of Arcadia.'

The Year Three unicorns grazing nearby looked up.

'Did Troy just say his dad's the king?' Willow heard one of them say. She nudged Troy and nodded towards the listening unicorns.

'It might have been hard to tell us,' Storm whispered to Troy, 'but you shouldn't have kept it secret from us.'

'You could have told us when we asked you what the Tricorn meant today,' Willow said in a low voice. 'You lied to us, Troy. You told us you didn't know.'

'I'm sorry, OK?' Troy burst out. 'I know I shouldn't have kept it secret, but I did! There's nothing I can do about it now.' Looking very upset, he galloped away.

The nearby unicorns whispered excitedly to each other and then trotted away to tell their friends the news.

Willow's heart sank. 'Oh dear, it looks like the whole school is soon going to know Troy's secret now,' she said to Storm.

'I hope it'll be OK for him,' said Storm.

Willow felt worried. 'Me too.'

Chapter
Five

New Friends

By teatime the news had spread through the school that Troy was a royal unicorn. Suddenly it seemed that everyone wanted to be his friend.

Willow, Storm and Sapphire watched Troy chatting to some of the Year Five and Six unicorns in the Moonlight Meadows before tea. The older unicorns all wanted to know things such as what his family's palace was like, how many stables it had, what sort of food he had to eat there, what his mum and dad were like. At first Troy looked embarrassed by all the attention, but soon he seemed to begin to enjoy it.

Willow was torn between wanting to go closer so she could hear the answers to the questions and wanting to ignore Troy because she was still cross with him.

'I guess Troy was right,' Storm said, looking at the unicorns surrounding him. 'People really do treat him differently.'

'He still should have told us,' said Willow. '*We* wouldn't have treated him differently – we're his friends.'

Just then the chief elf blew the shell for teatime. As the tables were brought out, the crowd of unicorns around Troy cleared a path for him to walk through. As he walked past Willow, Storm and Sapphire, he didn't meet their eyes.

'It seems that now he's told

everyone he's the prince we're not good enough for him any more,' Willow huffed.

Sapphire nuzzled her. 'Don't be silly, Willow. You know Troy's not like that. I bet he's just feeling guilty and embarrassed about not telling us.'

All the other unicorns stood back and Troy got to choose where he wanted to eat at the Rainbow House table. As soon as he had decided, the other unicorns jostled and pushed their way to the table, trying to get into one of the spaces beside him. Two Year Five unicorns who had been in the racing heats, Tiberius and Azure, got there first.

Azure smiled at him and Tiberius pulled over a bowl of extra carrots so that Troy could have first choice.

Willow, Storm and Sapphire ended up at the far end of the table. As she ate her tea of bran, barley and carrots, Willow watched Troy. He was talking to Azure and Tiberius about the heats that morning. They were telling him how well he had done in the heat and saying how he should have won it.

Willow sighed. It was strange eating with just Storm and Sapphire. They were quieter than Troy. Willow missed being able to tease him and having him tease her back. 'I wish Troy was sitting with us,' she said.

Sapphire nodded. 'It's not the same without him.'

'Let's try and talk to him after tea,' Storm suggested.

But after tea Azure and Tiberius stayed with Troy and didn't leave his side.

'If you like, you can practise flying with us tomorrow afternoon,' Willow heard Azure saying.

'I'd love to,' Troy replied, 'but I've promised to do something else already.' He glanced quickly at Sapphire, and Willow was sure he was thinking about the practice for Sapphire's birthday surprise.

Tiberius, a stocky white unicorn with a thick white mane and tail, looked surprised. 'But Azure and I never usually let any younger unicorns practise with us.'

'Um, well . . .' Troy looked torn. 'Maybe I *could* cancel what I was going to do,' he said slowly.

Willow couldn't believe her ears. She left Sapphire and Storm and trotted over. 'Troy!' she exclaimed. A look of guilt crossed Troy's face as he realized she'd overheard him.

'Troy, you're not really going to go flying tomorrow, are you?' Willow hissed, not wanting Sapphire to hear.

'Oh, yes he is,' said Azure. 'He just said so, didn't you, Troy?'

'Um . . . well . . .' Troy stammered. 'But what about practising for

Sapphire's birthday surprise?' Willow asked in a low voice.

'As if he'd do something babyish like that when he could be out flying with us,' said Tiberius scornfully.

'Come on, Troy. Let's go,' Azure said.

Azure and Tiberius flew into the sky. Troy hesitated.

'You can't miss the birthday practice tomorrow,' Willow said. 'It's Sapphire's birthday very soon.'

'It's only one practice,' Troy said.

'But it's important!' Willow stamped her hoof. 'First you keep secrets from us and now you won't come and practise for Sapphire's birthday party. I don't know why you bother being friends with us at all, Troy!'

'Me neither,' said Troy, looking upset, 'if that's how you feel!' He flew into the sky.

'Troy!' Willow exclaimed. But Troy ignored her and flew after Azure and Tiberius. Willow went slowly back to the others.

'What was that about?' Sapphire asked in surprise.

'Oh, nothing,' Willow muttered. 'We just had a bit of an argument.' She couldn't believe Troy had gone off like that.

I shouldn't have got so cross with him, she thought. *But he shouldn't have said he would miss the practice and he certainly shouldn't have kept secrets from us.*

She looked towards the Flying Heath. She could see Troy in the sky with Tiberius and Azure.

Storm nuzzled her. 'Don't worry about it. Come on, let's go to the beach. We'll see Troy later.'

★

But Troy stayed with Azure and Tiberius until it was bedtime. All the unicorns slept in stables in the clouds. The Year Ones had the lowest clouds, the Year Twos were above them and then the Year Threes, all the way up to the Year Sixes, who were at the very top. Each cloud was split into eight separate stalls. Windows were carved out of the cloud walls and the floor was soft and bouncy to walk on. Willow loved being in her cloud stable. It usually made her feel very happy and relaxed, but not that night. She couldn't stop thinking about the argument she'd had with Troy.

Troy eventually came into the stable. 'We haven't seen you since tea,' said Storm.

'I've been busy,' muttered Troy.

'Yes – hanging out with your new best friends,' said Willow. 'You know they only like you because you're the prince, Troy.'

'That's not true!' Troy retorted.

'It is so,' Willow replied. 'If they liked you for being you they'd have tried to make friends with you before they found out you were the prince.'

'I'm not listening. They said they're my friends! I'm going to sleep.' Troy lay down on the cloud bed and shut his eyes.

'Be like that then!' Willow snorted and lay down too.

'Night, everyone,' said Storm.

'Night,' said Sapphire.

Neither Willow nor Troy said a word.

Chapter Six

Azure and Tiberius

When Willow got up in the morning, she felt bad about the arguments the day before and wanted to make up with Troy, but when she looked over the partition that separated his stall from hers she found that he had already got up and left the stable. Looking out of her window, she saw him heading towards the Flying Heath.

I'll talk to him later, she thought.

But Troy avoided her and Storm and Sapphire. He went around with Azure and Tiberius all that day and the next. Soon they were hardly seeing him at all!

He ate with the older unicorns and hung around with them between lessons. If they were busy, he went to the Flying Heath and practised by himself for the flying race. He didn't turn up to any of the practices for Sapphire's birthday and at night-time he came into the stable and lay down without talking to anyone.

'I really miss Troy,' Sapphire said to Willow as they walked along the beach on Saturday. The Rose Quartz Cliffs glittered beside them, the pink rock sparkling in the sunlight. Sapphire had found a secret cave in the cliffs that she wanted to show Willow.

'I miss him too,' admitted Willow. 'I wish he still wanted to go around with us.'

'I think he does deep down. He's just feeling guilty about not telling us about being the prince,' said Sapphire.

'He doesn't have to stop being friends with us because of it,' Willow protested. 'And why does he hang around with Azure and Tiberius so much? They always seem to be bossing him about. I saw them yesterday making him fetch things from their stable for them. I don't understand why he does what they say.'

'Well, they are Year Fives,' Sapphire pointed out. 'And he probably thinks

it's cool to hang out with them.' She headed towards the cliff. 'The cave's just here, Willow.'

Willow followed Sapphire as she squeezed behind a rock and into a cave in the cliff wall. It was large enough for about five unicorns. There were rocks like icicles hanging from the ceiling and the walls gleamed softly in the dim light. Willow snorted. 'It's beautiful!'

'I love it!' Sapphire said. 'There are tunnels leading off it like secret passageways too!' She led the way down a tunnel and for twenty minutes the two of them had great fun exploring, using their unicorn magic to make their horns light up so they could see through the darkness.

They were just about to head back out on to the beach when they heard familiar voices near the cave entrance.

Willow stopped. 'It's Azure and Tiberius,' she said as she heard Troy's name mentioned.

'Troy's such a baby,' Azure was saying outside the cave.

'I know. But he is a prince so it is worth hanging out with him – even if he is just a Year One.' Tiberius laughed. 'He can be really stupid too. I asked him to give me a new blanket his mum had sent him to keep him warm at night and he did.'

'And he gave me his gold-plated mane comb when I said I'd lost mine,' said Azure. 'I'm going to tell him I've lost my body brush tonight and maybe he'll give me the one he has with the ruby in the handle.'

Willow felt hot anger rush through her. 'They're being so

mean!' she whispered. Sapphire nodded, her eyes worried.

'We should get him to invite us to the palace in the holidays,' said Azure. 'That would be so cool!'

'Yeah, it would be,' agreed Tiberius. 'Let's ask him tonight.'

'We'll tell him we won't be his friends any more if he doesn't invite us,' Azure said.

Tiberius sniggered. 'He'll have to invite us if we say that! Come on, let's go to the Flying Heath!' Then came the sound of their hooves trotting away on the sand.

Willow swung round to Sapphire. 'Did you hear what they said? They were being so horrid about Troy!'

'You were right – they only like him because he's the prince,' said Sapphire.

'We have to tell him!' said Willow.

They hurried out of the cave and found Troy by the stream in the Moonlight Meadows.

As they galloped over he started to move away. 'Wait, Troy!' Willow said. 'We need to talk to you.'

'It's about Azure and Tiberius,' Sapphire said. 'They aren't your real friends, Troy.'

'They just want stuff from you and to come and visit your palace,' Willow blurted out.

'We heard them talking,' Sapphire went on. 'They were saying how they keep getting you to give them things and that they were only friends with you because you're the prince.'

'I don't believe you!' Troy said, looking from one to the other.

'It's true!' Willow exclaimed.

Troy shook his head. 'No, I think you're just jealous because they want me to hang around with them. Well, I'm not going to listen to you being

horrid about my new friends!' He cantered off.

'Troy!' Sapphire called after him, but he didn't come back. 'What shall we do?' she said, turning to Willow.

'I don't know,' said Willow. She hated the thought that Azure and Tiberius were being so mean to Troy. She and Sapphire had to get him to listen to them, but how?

Chapter Seven

The Missing
Sash

The next morning was Sunday.
When Willow woke up she
poked her head over the partition
that separated her stall from
Sapphire's. 'Happy birthday!' she
whinnied.

Sapphire blinked and woke up.
'Thank you!' she said, pricking her ears.

Flint, Ash, Starlight and Topaz, the other Year One unicorns who shared the cloud stable, began to wake up and call *happy birthday* too.

Willow checked Troy's stall, but it was empty. She guessed he had gone out to get ready for the big race. *I hope I see him at the race*, she thought. Despite the arguments, she wanted to wish him good luck.

'Hey, look!' said Storm, noticing a parcel wrapped in silver paper at the entrance to Sapphire's stable. 'You've got a present, Sapphire. One of the elves must have delivered it.'

Sapphire read the tag. 'It's from my mum and dad and my brothers and sisters!'

She pawed the paper off with her hoof. 'Oh, wow!' she breathed. It was a star-shaped piece of glittering white quartz hanging from a long silver chain. Sapphire picked it up with her horn and slipped it over her head.

'It's beautiful,' Willow breathed.

Sapphire's eyes shone. 'I love it!' She touched the pendant with her muzzle and looked slightly wistful. 'I wish my family were here to do a birthday show for me,' she said. 'But I'm sure I'll still have a lovely day.'

'I bet you will,' Storm told her.

Willow felt slightly nervous. She hoped that she and Storm could make up for Sapphire's family not being there. They had been practising a lot, but it wasn't quite the same with just the two of them and no Troy. Two of them doing tricks didn't seem anything like as good as all three.

After breakfast they headed over to the Flying Heath. Most of the unicorns who were taking part in the race were already there.

'Troy looks worried about something,' Sapphire said to Willow and Storm.

Troy was looking round anxiously, his eyes scanning the crowds of watching unicorns as if he was looking for someone.

'Should we go and wish him
luck?' said Storm.

Willow nodded. 'Yes. Let's.' They
flew over.

'Hi, Troy!' Willow called.

'Oh, hi,' Troy said awkwardly. They
hadn't spoken since their row the
day before. 'Um, happy birthday,
Sapphire.'

'Thanks,' she said. 'Good luck today.'

'Where's your lucky sash?' Willow asked him as she suddenly realized that there was nothing round Troy's neck.

'Tiberius borrowed it yesterday,' Troy admitted. 'He said he'd bring it back to me before the race, but I haven't seen him.' He looked embarrassed. 'I know it's just some ribbons plaited together, but . . . well . . .'

'It's your lucky sash,' Willow said, understanding immediately.

Troy nodded. 'I don't want to race without it,' he said miserably.

'We could go and find Tiberius

for you,' Storm suggested, 'and ask him to give it back.'

'Will you really?' Troy asked, pricking his ears.

'Of course,' Storm told him. Willow and Sapphire nodded.

'Oh, thanks,' Troy said.

Willow smiled, glad they were all talking properly again. 'Come on!' she said to the others.

As they turned, Troy spotted Tiberius and Azure walking on to the heath. 'Look, there they are! They've brought it!'

The four of them all cantered over to the older unicorns, but the sash was nowhere to be seen. 'Where's my sash?' Troy asked them.

Tiberius looked puzzled. 'Your sash?'

'My lucky sash – the three ribbons plaited together,' said Troy.

'Oh, that old thing,' said Tiberius.

'Yes, but I need it for the race.'

Tiberius and Azure looked at each other. 'Ah, well, we kind of ripped it,' Azure admitted.

'You ripped it?' Troy echoed.

'Yeah, we were playing tag and I caught it with my teeth,' said Azure. 'But it was only a grotty old thing.'

Sapphire gasped.

'No, it wasn't!' Willow exclaimed. 'It was Troy's lucky sash. His mum made it!'

'Well, I'm sure she can buy him

another one,' said Tiberius. 'Or get one of the elves at the palace to make a replacement.'

'It won't be the same,' said Troy.

'And Troy needs it today,' put in Storm.

'Where is the sash?' asked Willow, wondering if there was time to go and mend it.

Azure shrugged. 'We chucked it in the bin.'

Troy caught his breath. 'In the bin!'

'Oh, get over it, Troy,' said Azure. 'It was just some stupid ribbons.'

Willow felt a wave of anger wash over her. Suddenly she didn't care that Azure and Tiberius were much older than she was. She stamped her hoof. 'You're both horrible!' she exclaimed. 'That sash meant a lot to Troy! If you were really his friends you'd see that. But you're not, are you? You're just pretending!'

Sapphire nodded vigorously. 'We heard you talking yesterday. You were saying you wanted to get Troy to give you things and that you were only friends with him because he's the prince!'

Troy stepped towards the older unicorns. 'It's not true, is it?'

'Of course it's not,' said Azure, but she couldn't quite meet Troy's eye.

'It *is* true, Troy!' said Sapphire.

Tiberius gave Troy a challenging

look. 'Who do you believe — us or them?'

Troy hesitated and then suddenly stepped back beside Willow, Sapphire and Storm. 'I believe them,' he declared firmly. Willow felt a wave of relief. She nuzzled Troy in delight.

Tiberius looked outraged. 'Well, don't think you can hang around with us any more!'

Troy lifted his head high. 'I don't want to. I don't want to be friends with you at all. I'd like all my things back, please, and you're not going to come to the palace in the holidays.'

'But you've already invited us,' protested Azure.

'Well, now you're *un*invited,' said Troy. 'Come on, everyone!' He swung round and cantered away.

'But . . . but . . .' Azure stammered. She and Tiberius looked stunned.

'See you later!' Willow grinned at them and raced after the others.

Troy stopped on the far side of the heath.

'You were brilliant, Troy!' exclaimed Storm.

Willow nudged him in delight. 'So cool!'

'Are you still my friends then?' Troy asked anxiously.

'Of course we are,' Sapphire replied and Storm nodded.

'But no secrets from now on,' said Willow.

Troy nodded. 'No secrets. I should have told all of you the truth much sooner.' He sighed. 'I'm really sorry about it and I'm sorry that I've been going around with Azure and Tiberius all week. I felt bad about not telling you that I was a prince, and Azure and Tiberius were really nice to me to start with, so it just seemed easier to hang around with them.' He looked round at them all. 'Would you all like to come and stay at the palace in the next holidays, instead of them?'

'Yes, please!' they all said in delight.

Just then there was the sound of a horn blowing. 'Would all the racing unicorns make their way over here, please!' called Atlas.

Troy looked alarmed. 'Oh, no! The race is about to start, but how can I compete without my lucky sash?'

'Troy, it's not your sash that makes you a good racer – it's being able to fly fast!' Willow told him. 'You can do it without your sash!'

'You've been practising loads this

week,' Storm put in. 'You'll be fine.'

Troy still looked uncertain.

'Here,' Sapphire said softly. She slipped her new necklace off, catching it with her silver horn. 'My mum and dad sent it to me for my birthday today. I know it's not your sash, but it's special to me and it might bring you luck.'

Troy stared at her. 'You'll really let me wear it?'

Sapphire nodded. 'Of course.' She placed it carefully over his head.

'Thank you,' Troy breathed, nudging it with his nose. 'Thank you *so* much,' he said, looking up at them all, his eyes shining. 'You're the best friends ever!'

'You're going to miss the race if you're not careful!' Willow told him.

'I'd better go,' gasped Troy.

'Good luck!' Sapphire, Storm and Willow whinnied as he galloped away.

Chapter Eight

The Race!

The unicorn racers all lined up. The whole school had come to watch. The Tricorn was standing behind a table with four medals on it. Willow, Storm and Sapphire were watching from the finish line.

'Good luck, Troy,' Willow whinnied as the chief elf slowly lifted the horn to his lips. The unicorns on the starting line fidgeted and jostled each other. They were the twelve fastest unicorns in the school – Juniper, Azure, Tiberius, Silver, Cloud, Neptune, Oriel, Midnight, Pearl, Apollo, Hera and Troy – and they were eager to be off.

The elf paused and then blew a sharp, clear note. As the unicorns plunged upward over the golden chain the watching crowd erupted into cheers. The race had begun!

Willow, Sapphire and Storm jumped up and down, whinnying Troy's name over and over again. The twelve unicorns galloped through the blue sky. They had to race round a

tree to the east of the heath and
a tree to the west and then it was a
gallop for the finish line.

As they hurtled round the second
tree Juniper was in the lead followed
by Silver, Neptune and Cloud. Azure
and Tiberius were neck and
neck behind them. But
Troy was close to them
and, though he was smaller
than the other unicorns,
he had a look of fierce
determination on his face.
'Troy's passing Azure
and Tiberius!'

Storm neighed as Troy pushed himself on.

'Go on, Troy!' yelled Willow in delight as Tiberius and Azure both faltered in surprise. There were just four unicorns ahead of Troy now, but the finish line was getting closer. He passed Silver and gained on the other three. Stride by stride he inched towards them.

'Faster, Troy!' Sapphire shrieked.

'You're almost there!' whinnied Storm.

Almost as though he had heard them, Troy tried even harder. He plunged forward, but the finish line came just too soon. Juniper crossed first, followed by Cloud and

Neptune, then Troy just a mane's hair behind them.

'He was fourth!' Sapphire gasped.

'That was brilliant!' said Storm.

'I hope Troy thinks so,' said Willow anxiously. 'You know how upset he was to come third last time.' Troy had landed beside the other unicorns and was panting for breath, his head down, his sides heaving with the effort he had just made.

'Let's go over and see him,' Storm said, but as he spoke Troy lifted his head and walked over to Juniper.

Though Troy was still panting, he congratulated the older unicorn. 'Well done on winning,' they heard him say.

Juniper thanked him and they

touched horns. Troy turned and breathlessly congratulated Neptune and Cloud too.

Willow felt a rush of pride. Good for Troy! She knew he would be really disappointed not to have won, but he seemed to have learnt his lesson from last time. She glanced quickly at the Tricorn. He was watching Troy and there was a smile on his face.

Troy came over to them.

'You did really well!' Willow told him.

'Thanks,' Troy said. 'I know I didn't win, but I tried my best.'

'And that's the most important thing,' said Storm.

'Not quite. The *most* important thing is having best friends like you three,' said Troy. He tipped the necklace over his head, passed it carefully back to Sapphire and then smiled at them all. 'Nothing is better than that.'

Just then the elf blew the horn. Silence fell. The Tricorn moved up behind the table. 'It is now time for the presentation of the medals,' he said. 'The gold medal goes to Juniper, the silver to Cloud and the bronze to Neptune.' The watching unicorns whinnied and stamped their hooves as the three prizewinners went up one at a time to collect their medals.

'There is one medal left,' the Tricorn said as the three winning unicorns stepped to one side. 'It is a medal for the best achievement. We award it every race. Atlas and I both agree that the winner today should be . . . Troy.'

'Me!' Troy gasped.

The Tricorn nodded at him. 'You have done very well to compete in your first unicorn race and come fourth when you are only a first year. Please come and collect your medal, Troy.'

Willow, Sapphire and Storm nudged him on. Troy walked to the table looking completely delighted.

'Congratulations,' the Tricorn said to him.

'Thank you,' Troy stammered.

'You did very well,' the Tricorn told him softly. 'Not just in coming fourth, but also in how you have behaved today. Your father will be very proud when I tell him, Troy.' He put the medal over Troy's head. Troy bowed and then cantered back to the others, a huge grin on his face.

'Well done,' Willow said.

'Thanks. Um, Willow?' Troy motioned with his head for her to move a little way away from the others. She followed him.

'Are you still doing a surprise birthday party for Sapphire?' said Troy in a low voice.

Willow nodded. 'Do you want to do it with us?' she asked hopefully.

'If you'll let me!' said Troy. 'I know I haven't been practising with you, but I've been doing so much flying this week I'm sure I'll be able to do the flying trick and I've got the cake. Although we weren't talking, I would have felt bad not getting it. Mum sent it to me. It's in the kitchens.'

'Brilliant!' said Willow. 'Why don't you and Storm collect it and take it down to the beach and I'll bring Sapphire there in about an hour?'

Troy nodded. 'OK! I'll put some decorations up and get a few of the others to come too.'

'But not Azure and Tiberius,' said Willow.

'No way!' Troy grinned. Willow looked towards the older two unicorns, who turned their backs huffily.

'I don't think they're talking to you,' said Willow.

'Who cares?' Troy said, swishing his tail. 'I'll go and get the cake.'

'See you at the beach!' said Willow.

Troy nodded. 'This is going to be the best birthday surprise ever!'

Willow kept Sapphire busy by insisting on going up to the stables and then saying she wanted to graze in Moonlight Meadows for a bit. Sapphire went with her and they found a patch of sweet grass near the edge of the meadows.

Sapphire was quiet as they grazed.

'Are you OK?' Willow asked her.

Sapphire nodded. 'I just feel a bit weird. It doesn't really seem like my birthday.' She touched her pendant with her muzzle. 'I love my present, but it's just not the same, having a birthday without a party.'

'Really?' Willow said. Sapphire nodded.

Willow smiled at her. 'Why don't we go down to the beach?' she said.

'OK,' Sapphire shrugged.

They headed towards the beach. As they walked on to the white sands Willow saw that a group of unicorns had gathered near the entrance to the secret cave. Silver and gold

streamers had been hung from the rocks, and on one large flat rock there was a huge pink and white iced cake almost as tall as Willow.

'What's going on?' Sapphire said in astonishment.

'*Surprise!*' Willow and the others whinnied in delight.

Storm and Troy came cantering over. 'Happy birthday, Sapphire!' they neighed.

'It's a party? For me?' Sapphire stammered.

Willow, Storm and Troy nodded. 'And not just any party,' said Willow. 'But one with magic tricks and birthday cake. Come on!'

She trotted towards the others.

Flint, Ash, Starlight and Topaz were there as well as Sapphire's friends Moondust, Ruby and Amber. They all gathered round, wishing Sapphire a happy birthday and giving her small gifts – lucky charms, plaited ribbons, pieces of rose quartz.

'And now it's time for the magic!' Willow announced.

She and Troy stepped out in front of the others. Storm went to stand by a nearby rock pool. Willow waved her horn in the air and a stream of sparkling red stars flashed out. She moved her horn in the shape of an 'H' as Storm touched his horn to the rock pool and made the water turn red. Troy galloped into the sky and flew high above them before diving down in an 'H' shape and then up again into an 'A', while Willow produced a stream of gold stars and Storm turned the water a glittering gold. The watching unicorns cheered as Willow and Troy began to spell out *Happy birthday, Sapphire!* in all the colours of the rainbow.

Troy finished his flying display with a swooping dive that brought him down to land perfectly in front of Sapphire.

Sapphire looked speechless with delight. 'Oh, thank you!' she gasped.

Willow and Storm cantered over

to join Troy. 'Did you like the magic?' Willow asked eagerly.

'It was brilliant!' said Sapphire. 'I always love my birthdays at home, but this really is the best birthday party ever!' She touched horns with them all. 'Thank you.'

'Let's have the cake!' said Troy.

Everyone gathered round the amazing cake. Willow hung back for a moment. The sea was lapping

against the white sands and behind them the Rose Quartz Cliffs were glittering in the sunlight. Willow tossed her mane happily. It was great being there with all her friends. She wondered what was going to be next for them all.

I don't know, she thought, *but I bet it's going to be fun!*